D0792030

YOU BAD DOG!

by Leslie Baker

DUTTON CHILDREN'S BOOKS
NEW YORK

CIP Data is available.

Published in the United States 2003 by Dutton Children's Books,
a division of Penguin Putnam Books for Young Readers
345 Hudson Street, New York, New York 10014
www.penguinputnam.com

Designed by Irene Vandervoort

First Edition
Manufactured in China
ISBN 0-525-47127-8
10 9 8 7 6 5 4 3 2 1

For Ellen,
Miss Beverly, and Ann

One day Bridget wanted to practice her snoozing.

But, as usual, her friend Lulu had other ideas.
"Here she comes again," Bridget sighed.

"Playtime," Lulu sang.
Bridget pretended to sleep.

"Playtime!" Lulu sang louder, right in Bridget's ear.
Bridget pretended to snore.

“PLAYTIME!!!” Lulu’s tail spun like a helicopter.

Before Bridget knew what was happening,
Lulu jumped on her…

hopped onto the table,
gobbled some cookies, and ran off.

"Uh-oh," said Bridget.

"YOU BAD DOG! OUTSIDE RIGHT NOW!"

Bridget was angry.
"That Lulu is always getting me into trouble."

Bridget went to her secret hiding place.
"Lulu will never find me here."

But before Bridget could shut her eyes,
Lulu's face appeared.

"Playtime!" Lulu ran in circles, trying to get Bridget to chase her.

“Stop that right now!” shouted Bridget.

But Lulu wouldn't stop.
Lulu had found fun.

Bridget had found trouble.

"YOU BAD DOG! SHOO!!"

That does it, Bridget thought.
I'm going to have to find a better hiding place.
She hurried toward town.

Soon she smelled something yummy. Popcorn!
She ducked into a building.

Inside, the floor was covered with treats.
Bridget moved up and down the aisles,
vacuuming up the goodies.

Stuffed and happy, she curled up
on a comfy seat for a nap.
With no Lulu in sight, she was soon dozing.

But not for long.
Bridget's eyes popped open as a movie suddenly began.
When music blared, she heard a familiar sound.
"Oh, no," she moaned.

Lulu was singing along.

"What's that howling?" someone asked.

"IT'S A DOG!"

"You've gone too far this time, Lulu!"
Bridget shouted. She leaped over the seats

and escaped before the door swung shut.
Lulu was trapped inside.

Alone at last, thought Bridget as she strolled slowly down the street.

She paused in front of an ice-cream shop.
She remembered being inside with Lulu once.
They had licked the cup clean together.

Bridget and Lulu did a lot of things together.

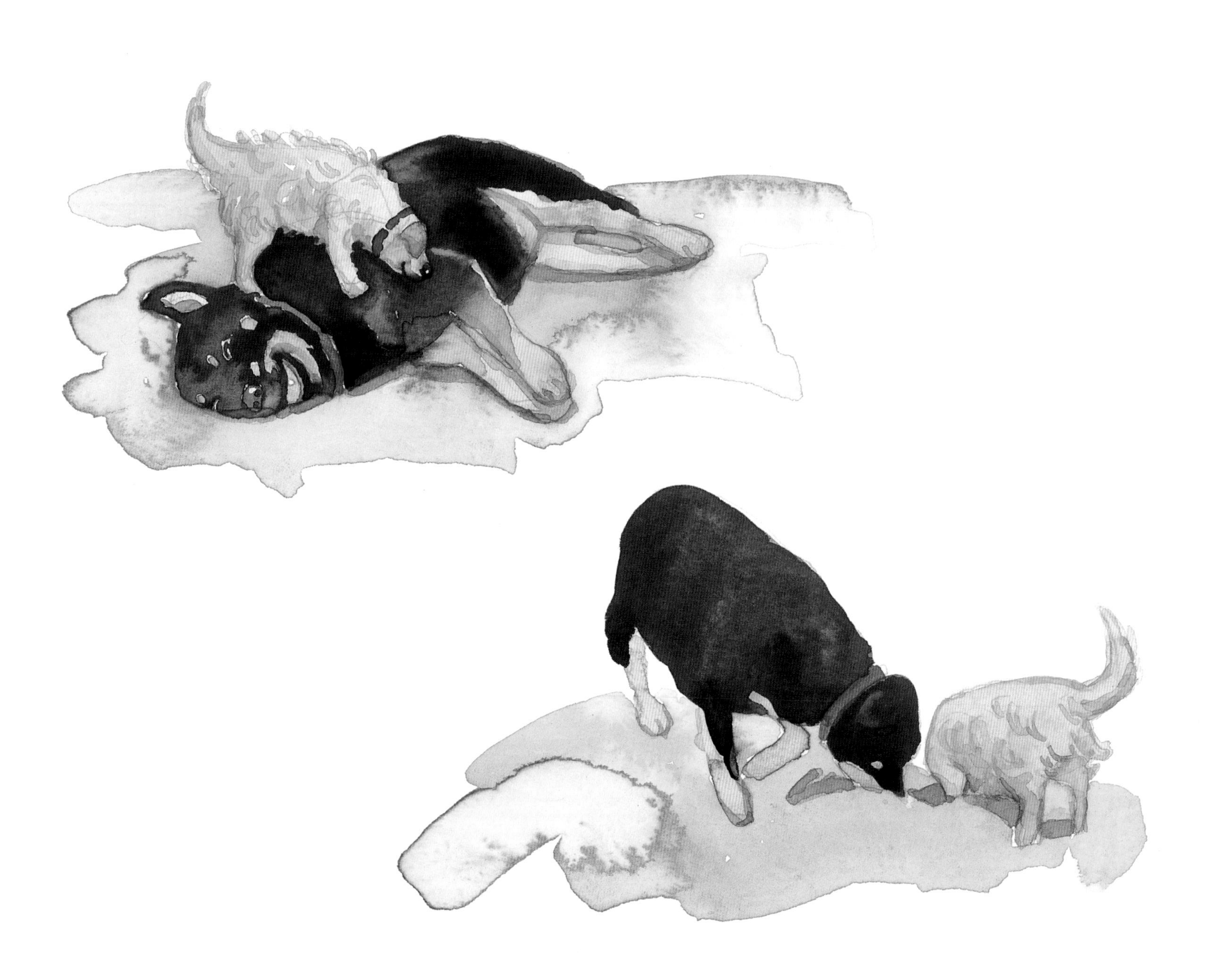

She knew she had to go back for Lulu.

She got there just in time.

"YOU BAD DOGS!"

On the way home, Bridget told Lulu that things would have to be different from now on.

Lulu licked Bridget's face.

Just then a cat ran across their path.
Bridget and Lulu looked at each other.

Lulu let out a happy bark and ran after the cat.
Bridget watched for a second.

"Playtime!" sang Bridget as she ran to join her friend.